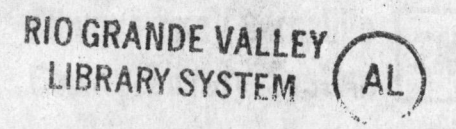

LOUIS
THE FISH

LOUIS
THE FISH

Story by Arthur Yorinks
Pictures by Richard Egielski
Farrar · Straus · Giroux
New York

For the Stoller family A. Y.

For Babci and Dziadzi R. E.

Text copyright © 1980 by Arthur Yorinks
Pictures copyright © 1980 by Richard Egielski
All rights reserved
Library of Congress catalog card number: 80–16855
Published in Canada by HarperCollinsCanadaLtd
Color separations by Offset Separations Corp.
Printed and bound in the United States of America by
Horowitz/Rae Book Manufacturers
Designed by Cynthia Krupat
First edition, 1980
Fourth printing, 1991

One day last spring, Louis, a butcher, turned into a fish. Silvery scales. Big lips. A tail. A salmon.

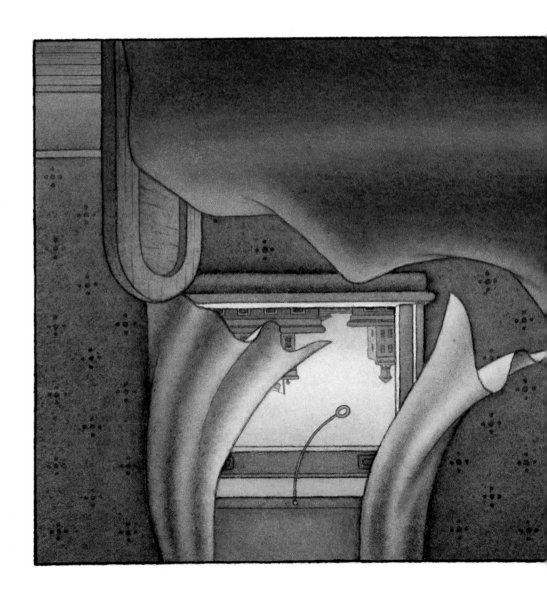

Louis did not lead, before this, an unusual life. His grandfather was a butcher. His father was a butcher. So, Louis was a butcher. He had a small shop on Flatbush. Steady customers. Good meat. He was always friendly, always helpful, a wonderful guy.

But Louis was not a happy man. He hated meat. From the time he was a little boy he was always surrounded by meat. Whenever he would visit his grandfather on Sundays it was always, "Louis, my favorite grandson. What a good boy. Here's a hotdog." On his birthdays his beaming parents would hand him a gift-wrapped salami. When he was thirteen they gave him a turkey.

Louis did anything to get away from meat. He got a job, afternoons, cleaning fish tanks in a doctor's office. Louis loved the job. For hours he'd stare at the fish, their eyes blinking, their fins flapping. But a good thing doesn't last long.

One night at dinner, Louis's mother said to his father: "Nat, why does Louis have to slave over those lousy fish? What's the matter? You can't give him a little job in the store?"

"But, Ma, I like—"

"You're right, Rose. Tomorrow, Louis, after school, you come to the store. It's time you learned something about meat."

And that was it. Every day Louis was at his father's shop. "Someday this will all be yours," his father would say.

And it was. His parents died suddenly and Louis took over the butcher shop. For years that's where he worked.

Louis was so unhappy. His only happy times were when he was in the refrigerator. There he'd sit for hours and draw fish. Big ones. Little ones. He'd draw them all over the place. Surrounded by steaks, all Louis thought about was fish. But then it got worse.

He began to see fish everywhere. At home. On the
bus. At ball games. Even his customers began to look
like fish to him.

Business started to fail. His health declined. He was
always thirsty.

At night Louis had trouble sleeping. One night in May, he had bad dreams. He dreamt he was walking down the street and he was attacked. Hamburgers were punching him. Salamis kicked him. Lamb chops, roast beefs, and briskets all ganged up on him. He yelled for help, but no one came.

That morning Louis woke up feeling cold and wet. He was a fish. A salmon.

Al, from Al's Pet Store, found him on the bus going up Flatbush.

"Look at that face," he tells his customers. "I couldn't eat him, so I brought him to the store."

Louis soon forgot everything about being a butcher, living on Flatbush, or even being a human being at all.

After a hard life, Louis was a happy fish.